PIKACHU IN LOVE

Adapted by Tracey West

Scholastic Inc.

New York   Toronto   London   Auckland   Sydney

Mexico City   New Delhi   Hong Kong   Buenos Aires

ISBN 0-439-42990-0

20 19 18 17 16   8/0

Printed in the U.S.A.
First printing, January 2003

Ash and his friends always meet strange
Pokémon on their adventures.

But one day, they met a strange
person. Pikachu was surprised.

"I am Old Man Shuckle," said the little man. "I make special medicine for Pokémon."

"*Pika?*" asked Pikachu.

"How do you do that?" Brock asked.

"It's a secret," said Old Man Shuckle. "I use a Pokémon called Shuckle."

"Please tell me!" Brock begged.

Old Man Shuckle explained each step.

First, he put secret ingredients inside the Shuckle shell.

Then he let the Shuckle loose in the wild.

A year later, he found the Shuckle again.
Then he took the juice out of the shell.

"There is even a special kind of juice that can make any Pokémon easy to catch and train," said the old man. "To make it, you must use a rare blue Shuckle."

"Easy-to-train Pokémon!" Brock said. "If I had that juice, I could become the world's best Pokémon trainer."

"I can give you some of that juice," said Old Man Shuckle. "But you and your friends must help me."

Old Man Shuckle called for his
Bellsprout.

"This is Spoopie," he said.
"Spoopie can sniff out wild Shuckle. I
need you to follow Spoopie and
collect the blue Shuckle for me."

"We'll help!" said Brock. Ash and Misty agreed.

"*Pika!*" said Pikachu.

"*Togi, togi,*" said Togepi.

The friends followed Spoopie into the woods.

Spoopie sniffed the air. Then it began to run.

"That Spoopie is very speedy!" said Misty.

They all chased Spoopie through the woods.

Spoopie found lots of Shuckle. It threw the Shuckle in the air for the others to catch.

"It's like a Shuckle shower!" Ash cried.

Then Spoopie ran off again.

"Slow down, Spoopie!" Brock called out.

Spoopie sniffed and sniffed.
It found the rare blue Shuckle!

Suddenly, Team Rocket dropped down
from the trees.

"The blue Shuckle is ours now!"
Jessie cried.

"Weezing, use Smoke Screen!" James yelled.

Thick smoke filled the air.

Team Rocket was gone!

Team Rocket ran and ran.

"I am thirsty!" Jessie said.

Team Rocket did not have water. They drank the juice from the blue Shuckle!

Meowth felt a little strange.
"I love you, James!" Meowth said.

Then it gave James a big hug and a kiss.

Nearby, the wild Shuckle began to move.
"Where are they going?" Ash asked.

"Someone drank the blue Shuckle juice," Old Man Shuckle said. "You should not drink it right from the shell. If you do, it makes Pokémon fall in love with you!"

The Shuckle were all in love with Jessie.
They licked her face.

"Yuck!" Jessie yelled. She ran away.

Team Rocket ran right into Ash and his friends.

"Give that blue Shuckle back right now!" Misty said.

"We will fight you first!" Jessie said. She called on Wobbuffet and Arbok.

But the Pokémon did not want to fight.

They wanted to hug Jessie!

"Great!" Ash said. "Pikachu, use Thunderbolt!"

But Pikachu did not attack. It was in love with Jessie, too!

Old Man Shuckle ran up.

"This has gone too far!" he said.

He sprinkled a powder on all of the Pokémon.

"The powder has cured the Pokémon," he said.

He was right. The Pokémon were not in love with Jessie and James anymore.

Spoopie made the first move.

It used Vine Whip to take the blue
Shuckle from Jessie's arms.

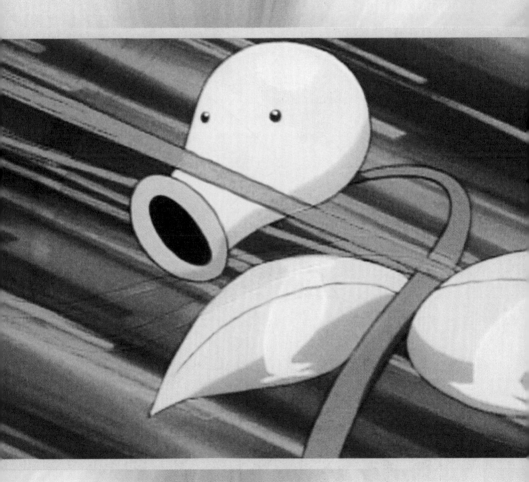

"We still have Pikachu," Jessie bragged.

But Pikachu was not in love with Jessie anymore.

"Pikachuuuuuuu!"

Pikachu shocked Team Rocket. They went blasting off again.

"Thank you for finding the blue Shuckle, Brock," Old Man Shuckle said. "Here is the special juice I promised you. You can use it to catch and train any Pokémon."

"No thanks," Brock said. "I want Pokémon to love me for who I am. Not because of any juice."

"I think they already do," Ash said.

"*Pika!*" Pikachu agreed.